252082

You're all Animals

First published in 2000

1 3 5 7 9 10 8 6 4 2

First published in the United Kingdom in 2000 by
Hutchinson Children's Books
The Random House Group Limited
20 Vauxhall Bridge Road, London SW1V 2SA

Random House Australia (Pty) Limited
20 Alfred Street, Milsons Point, Sydney
New South Wales 2061, Australia

Random House New Zealand Limited
18 Poland Road, Glenfield
Auckland 10, New Zealand

Random House South Africa (Pty) Limited
Endulini, 5A Jubilee Road, Parktown 2193, South Africa

The Random House Group Limited Reg. No. 954009

www.randomhouse.co.uk

A CIP catalogue record for this book
is available from the British Library

ISBN: 0 09 176797 0

Printed in Hong Kong

You're all Animals
Nicholas Allan

HUTCHINSON
London Sydney Auckland Johannesburg

I went to my new school
on Monday.

'This is Billy Trunk,' said Teacher.

Everyone smiled. But I didn't like them.
They were all different.
There was no one like me.

One had teeth all
down his nose...

One was slimy...

One was spotty...   and one smelt
                           really bad.

I wouldn't talk to any of them.

When I got home I told Mum and Dad.
'I want a friend who's just like me.'

'I know,' said Dad. 'Let's see
if we can find one
on the computer.'

So Dad typed:

MY NAME'S
BILLY TRUNK.
I'M 7 AND I LIKE
SKATEBOARDING.

The next day at school I had to do
P.E. with someone with weird arms.

When I got home Dad turned on the computer.

'Wow! Frank sounds just like me!'

So I typed:

The next day at school I had to sit at lunch
with someone who ate strange food
with a dribble-tongue.

I couldn't wait to get home.

'Wow! Frank's just like me!'

So I typed:

The next day at school someone sat down beside me who I thought was really creepy.

When I got home:

So then I typed:

Next morning:

'That Frank is just like me!'

I ran to school. I couldn't wait to meet Frank.
At last I had a friend who was just like me.

When I got there I looked and looked.
I couldn't see Frank anywhere.

But just then I heard a voice
call out, 'Watcha, Billy!'

I turned, and that's when I saw
my great friend Frank, who I already
knew for sure was just like me!